Teggs is no ordinary dinosaur –
he's an **ASTROSAUR!** Captain of
the amazing spaceship DSS *Sauropod*, he
goes on dangerous missions and fights
evil – along with his faithful crew,
Gipsy, Arx and Iggy!

Collect all the **ASTROSAURS!**
Free collector cards in every book for
you to swap with your friends.

For more astro-fun visit the website
www.astrosaurs.co.uk

www.**randomhousechildrens**.co.uk

Find out more at www.stevecolebooks.co.uk

Astrosaurs

THE TWIST OF TIME

Steve Cole

Illustrated by Woody Fox

RED FOX

THE TWIST OF TIME
A RED FOX BOOK 978 1 849 41895 9

First published in Great Britain by Red Fox,
an imprint of Random House Children's Publishers UK
A Random House Group Company

This edition published 2010

The Random House Group Limited supports The Forest Stewardship Council
(FSC®), the leading international forest certification organisation. Our books
carrying the FSC label are printed on FSC® certified paper. FSC is the only forest
certification scheme endorsed by the leading environmental organisations,
including Greenpeace. Our paper procurement policy can
be found at www.randomhouse.co.uk/environment

Typeset in Bembo MT Schoolbook

Red Fox Books are published by Random House Children's Publishers UK,
61–63 Uxbridge Road, London W5 5SA

www.**randomhousechildrens**.co.uk
www.**randomhouse**.co.uk

Addresses for companies within The Random House Group Limited can
be found at: www.randomhouse.co.uk/offices.htm

THE RANDOM HOUSE GROUP Limited Reg. No. 954009

A CIP catalogue record for this book is available from the British Library.

Printed and bound by CPI Group (UK) Ltd, Croydon, CR0 4YY

For Ruth Knowles
Who gamely twists time around
my deadlines

WARNING!

THINK YOU KNOW ABOUT DINOSAURS?

THINK AGAIN!

The dinosaurs . . .

Big, stupid, lumbering reptiles. Right?

All they did was eat, sleep and roar a bit. Right?

Died out millions of years ago when a big meteor struck the Earth. Right?

Wrong!

The dinosaurs weren't stupid. They may have had small brains, but they used them well. They had big thoughts and big dreams.

By the time the meteor hit, the last dinosaurs had already left Earth for ever. Some breeds had discovered how to travel through space as early as the Triassic period, and were already enjoying a new life among the stars.

No one has found evidence of dinosaur technology yet. But the first fossil bones were only unearthed in 1822, and new finds are being made all the time. The proof is out there, buried in the ground.

And the dinosaurs live on, way out in space, even now. They've settled down in a place they call the Jurassic Quadrant and over the last sixty-five million years they've gone on evolving . . .

The dinosaurs we'll be meeting are

 part of a special group called the Dinosaur Space Service. These heroic herbivores are not just dinosaurs.

They are *astrosaurs*!

NOTE: The following story has been translated from secret Dinosaur Space Service records. Earthling dinosaur names are used throughout, although some changes have been made for easy reading. There's even a guide to help you pronounce the dinosaur names on the next page.

Talking Dinosaur!

How to say the prehistoric
names in this book . . .

STEGOSAURUS –
STEG-oh-SORE-us

BAROSAURUS –
bar-oh-SORE-us

HADROSAUR –
HAD-roh-sore

IGUANODON –
ig-WA-noh-don

ALLOSAUR –
AL-uh-SORE

DIMORPHODON –
die-MORF-oh-don

TRICERATOPS –
try-SERRA-tops

THE CREW OF THE DSS SAUROPOD

**CAPTAIN
TEGGS STEGOSAUR**

ARX ORANO,
FIRST OFFICER

GIPSY SAURINE,
COMMUNICATIONS
OFFICER

IGGY TOOTH,
CHIEF ENGINEER

Jurassic Quadrant

Ankylos

Steggos

Diplox

INDEPEND
DINOSA
ALLIAN

vegetarian sector

Squawk
Major

DSS UNION OF PLANETS

PTEROSAUR

Tri System

Corytho

Lambeos

C

Iguanos

Aqua Minor

SEA

OUTER SPACE

Geldos Cluster

Teerex Major

TYRANNOSAUR

Olympus

carnivore sector

Raptos

Planet Sixty

THEROPOD EMPIRE

Megalos

vegmeat zone
(neutral space)

E SPACE

Pliosaur Nurseries

Not to scale

THE TWIST OF
TIME

Chapter One

TOP-SECRET TEST

Teggs Stegosaur strode across the asteroid's icy surface in full combat gear. The torch in his special helmet lit his way through the darkness. Heaters in his chunky metal suit protected him from the freezing cold. As Teggs headed into the unknown, he checked that his

leg lasers were loaded, his breastplate blasters were good to go and his tail cannon was fully charged . . .

Because hiding somewhere on this dim and distant space rock were twenty of the toughest robot T. rexes in the universe!

"DSS Headquarters to Captain Teggs." The voice of Admiral Rosso, the crusty old barosaurus in charge of the

Dinosaur Space Service, burst from Teggs's helmet. "Are you receiving me?"

"I certainly am, sir," Teggs replied. He was a dashing, orange-brown stegosaurus — and right now, he was very, very excited. He and the crew of his amazing ship, the DSS *Sauropod*, had been hand-picked to test a top-secret range of brand new, super-swish space battle armour! "Are the space cameras

4

sending their pictures OK?" asked Teggs.

"They're working fine," said Rosso happily. "The picture's so clear, it's hard to believe you're really billions of miles away. I have an excellent view of the whole asteroid, and I'm ready to record all the action. How does the new armour feel?"

"Fantastic!" Teggs glanced down at the glittering gold creation – it made him feel more like a walking tank than a dinosaur! "It's strong, but incredibly light."

"Most of it's made from maxi-strength mega-metal," Rosso explained. "One of the oldest, purest and hardest substances in the Jurassic Quadrant."

"Cool." Teggs smiled. "But what's even cooler is the built-in snack dispenser!"

"Our DSS designers think of everything," Rosso agreed. "They know you're always hungry – for food *and* action!"

"True." Teggs smiled and chomped on a mouthful of ferns. "Well, there's no sign of the robo-rexes yet, sir. But I can't wait to tackle them."

"Be very careful, Teggs," said Rosso sternly. "Our boffins designed those robots to test the new armour to its limits. They are programmed to squash, splat, stomp and squish you – and they will show no mercy!"

"Understood," Teggs said. "I'll check in with the gang and see how they're getting on in *their* armour. Teggs out!" He pressed a button on his communicator. "Teggs calling Arx. Can you hear me?"

Arx, Teggs's clever second-in-command, came back to him straight away. "Actually, Captain, I can *see* you as well. My battle-suit lets me fly!"

Teggs looked up and saw a gleaming, four-legged figure come zooming down out of the sky. Arx was a green triceratops, although you wouldn't know that right now – he looked more like a dino-knight in shining silver armour. The moulded metal fit around him like a second skin, and his three horns were plugged into powerful electro-blasters.

"I've scouted round sector one of the asteroid," Arx reported. "No sign of the robo-rexes."

"They aren't here in sector two, either," said Teggs. He flicked on his communicator. "Anything to report, Gipsy?"

"I can see something, Captain!" Gipsy

cried. The stripy hadrosaur was a brilliant officer and one of his best friends. "Oh, hang on – it's just you and Arx. I didn't recognize you in your space armour."

Teggs and Arx turned to find Gipsy waving from the crest of a rocky hill. Her purple, spiky armour was made of super-tough rubber. "Have you found any robo-rexes in sector three?" Teggs called to her.

Gipsy shook her head – then jumped into the air and came bouncing down the slope towards them like a spiky ball. "This is the best combat suit ever," she said, landing neatly in front of them. "I'm dying to test it out properly against the robots."

Teggs smiled as he spoke again into his suit's communicator. "Iggy, are you there?"

"I've searched sector four, Captain," said Iggy – a tough iguanodon who was a whizz with engines and machines. "I reckon these test-robots must be invisible. All I've found are a couple of long, thin cracks in the ground."

"Hmm," said Teggs, checking Iggy's position on the electronic space map inside his helmet. "Wait there, Ig – we're coming to join you." He looked at Arx and grinned. "Any chance of a lift?"

Arx smiled back and stretched out his armoured tail. "Grab on!"

Gipsy curled back into a big, spiky

ball. "I'll switch to mega-bounce mode and follow you."

Arx's foot jets flamed into life. Teggs was soon rising up with him into the night sky and Gipsy rolled along beneath them. But as he swung from the triceratops's tail, Teggs felt a moment's unease. They had come here to the edge of space so no one could spy on the tests. But if anything went wrong, help was a very long way away – even for the *Sauropod*'s mighty engines.

"There's Iggy now," Arx called, pointing an armoured foot.

"And those must be the cracks in the ground," Teggs noted. They ran side-by-side, like the rails on a train track.

Iggy saw his friends approaching and saluted in his bright red, chunky armour. The two robotic tentacles attached to his armour saluted too! "These extendable auto-grippers are amazing," Iggy enthused. "All I have to do is think and they move and stretch all by themselves." To prove it, he wrapped the tentacles round Gispy. "See?"

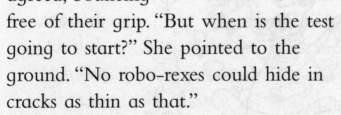

"We've all got brilliant armour," Gipsy agreed, bouncing free of their grip. "But when is the test going to start?" She pointed to the ground. "No robo-rexes could hide in cracks as thin as that."

Arx gasped as the long slice of icy ground suddenly exploded into the air. "But they *could* be hiding underground in the space BETWEEN the cracks!"

A deadly rain of frozen rock

threatened to crush the astrosaurs – but Iggy used his tentacles to bash the falling bits away. Then suddenly, twenty robo-rexes jumped out from the crevice in the asteroid's crust! They were giant, steel monsters with crushing claws, guns galore and lasers for eyes. Without a moment's pause, they opened fire on the astrosaurs.

Teggs gasped as he was smashed to the ground. He'd never seen such

powerful robots. *Test or not,* he thought, *these robots will fight us to the death . . .*

"Into battle!" roared Teggs.

One of the robo-rexes blasted Gipsy with a white-hot laser beam. But it only had time to singe a single spike before she boldly bounced towards the robot and knocked it flat.

Another fired bombs at Teggs, but his suit kept him safe. He let rip with his tail cannon and blew off the robot's bottom! The creature collapsed with a clanging crash, but two more stomped forward to take its place.

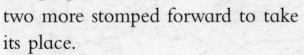

Meanwhile, Arx charged at the nearest robotic T. rex and fried its circuits with his electro-horns, while Iggy wrapped his auto-grippers around two of the metal monsters and smashed their heads together. Sparks flew from their electronic ears. "Cool!" cried Iggy.

But suddenly, something large, round and dark swooped overhead through the starry sky. Teggs looked up from the battle to find a spaceship hovering above them, marked with a sinister scarlet skull – the mark of meat-eaters. "Guys, look out!" he shouted. "We've got *real* carnivore company . . ."

While Teggs was distracted, a robo-rex lunged forwards and booted him through the air with its turbo-powered toes! He landed with a crunching clatter halfway up a nearby hillside. Iggy, Arx and Gipsy raced over to check he was all right. The remaining robo-rexes marched after them.

As they did so, Teggs saw a dark figure lean out from inside the spaceship with something that looked like a bucket . . .

And in the blink of an eye, the robo-rexes fell to pieces! All that remained of the massive monsters were several big piles of plastic and metal, surrounded by circuits, screws and springs.

"Great galaxies," Teggs cried, as Arx, Iggy and Gipsy helped him up. "What happened?"

"Ha, ha, ha!" The deep, rasping chuckle boomed out from the carnivore ship. "Sorry, astrosaurs – we seem to have spoiled your little workout. Does that make you mad? Well then, why not come and catch us – if you can!"

Chapter Two

CHASE THROUGH THE STARS

Gipsy glared up angrily at the carnivore craft as it slowly circled through the skies above them. "What do those miserable meat-eaters want? Do you think they're after our secret space armour?"

"I'm not sure," said Teggs. "They destroyed those super-tough robots – they could do the same to us. But instead they want us to *chase* them."

"Well, you plant-eating pant-heads?" the deep, growling voice came again from the carnivore ship. "Are you afraid to come after us, or what?"

Iggy bunched his armour's grippers so they made a massive club. "Come down here and say that."

Teggs fired his tail cannon at the spaceship – but the carnivores steered higher into the air, just out of range. "Missed us!" they jeered.

"Attention, astrosaurs." Suddenly, Admiral Rosso's voice boomed through the speakers in their armour. "DSS computers confirm that the craft above you is a warship from the planet Allosauria."

"Then there are allosaurs on board?" Gipsy's head-crest had turned blue with alarm – and Teggs couldn't blame her.

Allosaurs were massive, savage brutes who made even raptors look kindly in comparison.

"I didn't know the allosaurs had weapons as powerful as that," said Teggs.

"I didn't know *anyone* did," Rosso admitted.

"COME AND GET US, YOU ASTRO-PLOPS!" roared the voice from the ship. "OR WE WILL BLOW YOUR SPACESHIP TO BITS!"

"No one threatens the *Sauropod* and gets away with it," Teggs declared. "If it's a chase these allosaurs want, they're going to get one. Let's go!"

"Take care, Teggs," said Rosso. "I don't know how the allosaurs have learned about this top-secret test site, but something tells me there's more to their attack than meets the eye."

"We'll find out what, sir," said Teggs, "and that's a promise. To the *Sauropod* – NOW!"

The four astrosaurs raced away to their giant, egg-shaped ship, which was parked half a mile away. Arx arrived first in his flying suit, towing Teggs behind him.

Iggy used his metal tentacles like giant legs to stride across the asteroid, while Gipsy rolled along like a big purple bowling ball.

"At last," came the harsh roar. The allosaur warship whizzed away from the little rock, heading for the starry depths of space . . .

Once aboard the *Sauropod*, Teggs led the rush for the flight deck and jumped into his control pit. CRRRUNCH! His armour made him too big to fit, and he got wedged between the sides. The *Sauropod*'s fifty-strong flight crew of dazzling dino-birds – the dimorphodon – flapped down to take off his helmet and try to lift him free.

"Thanks, guys, but there's no time right now," Teggs told them. "We must follow that spaceship that just took off from here."

As Arx, Iggy and Gipsy took their places in the flight deck – with some difficulty – the dimorphodon squealed

and banged buttons with their beaks and claws. There was a smoky rumble of heavy-duty thrusters, and then the *Sauropod* blasted off from the bleak asteroid.

Arx checked his space radar. "The allosaur ship is already five thousand miles away," he reported. "Headed for uncharted space."

"Uncharted by us, anyway," Teggs muttered. "Increase speed to maximum." With a powerful roar, the *Sauropod* streaked away through space at ten million miles per hour. "Those allosaurs mustn't escape!"

"They *could* have got away the

moment they ruined our robots," Arx reminded him. "Instead, they waited *for* us."

"Do you think they're up to something?" Gipsy worried.

"Whatever it is, they'll be sorry," said Iggy. "We're catching them up."

"Launch two dung torpedoes," Teggs commanded. "NOW!"

Pa-CHOW! Pa-CHOW! The whiffy weapons shot out from the *Sauropod*. Seconds later, two stinky brown explosions bloomed on the side of the allosaur ship.

"Two hits!" Iggy reported. "We've smashed their shields!"

Arx was still peering at his space radar. "And it looks like we've knocked them off course. They're zooming towards the nearest sun." He paused. "No, wait. There's a tiny planet there too."

"But are they heading there because we've damaged their ship?" Iggy wondered. "Or were they trying to lead us to that planet all the time?"

Teggs chomped worriedly on a twig. "You think it's a trap?"

"Could be," said Arx.

"Message coming through, Captain." Gipsy flicked a switch. "It's Admiral Rosso."

"Teggs?" the

admiral called urgently. "You've flown out of range of our space cameras. What's happening?"

Teggs quickly explained the situation.

"We *must* discover what destroyed those robots," Rosso declared. "A weapon like that could spell doom for the entire Vegetarian Sector."

"Don't worry, sir," said Teggs. "We'll follow the allosaurs and find out all we can." He scraped his way out of the control pit and gave his team a crooked smile. "We wanted to test this space armour − looks like it's time to try it out for real!"

Chapter Three

LITTLE PROBLEMS

Teggs, Gipsy, Arx and Iggy squeezed inside a shuttle and flew down to the barren little world. There wasn't much to see beyond bright red sandy deserts and orange rocky cliffs. But there was something sinister about the place. Caves and chasms were dotted about the planet's surface, like dark mouths screaming beware.

Teggs gave his crew a reassuring smile. "As soon as we find out what the allosaurs are up to, we'll signal the *Sauropod* to send in reinforcements."

Gipsy checked the controls – and gasped. "I don't think we'll be able to," she said. "The shuttle's communicator has stopped working."

"Try the communicators in your armour, everyone," said Teggs. But it soon became clear that they weren't working either.

"We're too close to that giant sun," Arx realized. "Solar radiation must be scrambling the signals."

"We'll just have to fly back to the

Sauropod if we need any help," said Iggy brightly.

Teggs nodded. *On a tiny ship with no communicator at the edge of known space*, he thought nervously. *If anything bad happens on this planet, we're on our own.*

Iggy flew the shuttle all the way around the tiny world. "No sign of the carnivore ship anywhere," he said.

"Wait a moment," said Gipsy, pointing through the windscreen. "What's that?"

Bumping together in their armour, the other astrosaurs leaned forward to see. There was a big pile of metal, plastic and bits of junk lying on a rocky plain.

"There were similar bits and pieces left behind when the robo-rexes got destroyed," Teggs remembered. "Perhaps the allosaurs' secret weapon dismantles machines — and they accidentally set it off when they crash-landed?"

As soon as the shuttle was down, Teggs and his team ventured out onto the baking hot planet. The sun was bright and scorching in the sky. Keeping cool in their armour despite the fierce heat, they approached the scattered piles of parts.

"There's no sign of any allosaurs," Teggs observed. "I wonder what happened to them?"

"*I* wonder why there's no sign of an actual crash," said Gipsy. "There's no crater, no marks - nothing but metal and plastic and about a million spare parts."

Arx nodded. "It's like someone simply took apart the entire spaceship."

"And gave it a really good clean at the same time," Iggy added. He held up a large metal tube. "This has come from the dung-burners. It ought to be scorched and covered in dung-soot. Instead, it's like new." He waved his auto-grippers around the crash site. "*All* these parts are like new – except for this power piston. It's the only thing that looks like it's seen some space action."

Arx had a look. "It's made of mega-metal," he noted. "Like the captain's armour."

Teggs hardly heard them, deep in thought. "Something very strange is going on around here."

Then suddenly, a high-pitched, giggling growl sounded from nearby.

"What's that?" asked Gipsy nervously.

Teggs pointed to a small hole in a nearby hillside. "It sounded like it came from in there . . ."

The next moment, a small, dark green dinosaur came scuttling out of the hole. It had small arms and sharp claws. Its eyes were big, and its teeth even bigger. It stared round at the armoured astrosaurs, wagging its tail.

"I don't get it." Iggy stared at the dinosaur. "It looks like an allosaur. But it's about ten times too small."

"It's almost *cute*," Teggs admitted.

The dinosaur turned back to the little cave and called in a squeaky voice. "Hey, everyone, look! Funny-coloured monsters. Look!"

Seconds later, another near-identical dinosaur came out, followed by another, and another. There were maybe thirty all together. They "ooohed" and "ahhhed" at the sight of the astrosaurs and started running about with their tails wagging.

"I think they're *baby* allosaurs,"

breathed Gipsy. "What in space would babies be doing on an allosaur warship?"

"Crying, weeing and pooing a lot, I expect," joked Iggy.

One of the tots jumped up to Teggs. "What you funny monsters doing here?" it asked.

"We've just dropped in." Teggs stooped down in his armour and gave the allosaur nippers his friendliest smile. "Where are your mums and dads?"

"Us not got mums and dads," one baby replied.

"Someone must look after you." said Gipsy.

"Other funny monsters leave water sometimes," the baby replied. "Water and stale biscuits. YUK!"

"Other funny monsters?" Teggs frowned.

"Us think them is skinny and chewy-looking," said another nipper, waddling up to Teggs. "But you look fat and juicy. Me gonna . . . EAT YOU!"

And suddenly it pounced on Teggs's back, biting at his armour. "Hey!" Teggs cried, rearing up. "Get off!"

"Save some for us!" said another toddler. It jumped onto Teggs's helmet, scratching the glass visor with its claws.

"Let's eat the purple thing!" cried an allosaur tyke, hurling itself onto Gipsy.

"Don't be so naughty!" Gipsy told it. But already, more and more allosaurs were swarming over her, chomping on her rubbery spikes with razor sharp teeth. "Oh, no! Help!"

"I want to eat the *silver* monster!" An over-excited infant leaped onto Arx's side and started ripping through the rivets holding his helmet to his metal suit.

"This is terrible," Arx groaned, trying to shake the allosaur free. "We can't fight baby carnivores, no matter how rotten they are!"

"Hang in there," said Iggy, trying to

keep more toddlers at bay with his auto-grippers. "Maybe they'll get tired in a minute . . ."

"Tired! Of course!" cried Teggs. "If we sung these little devils a lullaby, it might just make them sleep. Iggy, do you know any?"

"Er . . ." Iggy racked his brains, trying to remember an old carnivore poem he'd once read. "How about this? *Rock-a-bye raptor, on a loose brick. You are so ugly, you make me feel sick!*"

One of the little allosaurs started to slide drowsily off of Gipsy. "It's working!" she hissed.

Teggs nodded as the tot on his helmet started yawning. "Keep going!"

Iggy sang softly: "*Rotten old raptor, I'll put you to bed. And stick my sick-bucket right over your head!*" He crooned the song again, softer, slower, until every one of the baby allosaurs had dozed off, snoring contentedly.

"Phew!" Gipsy whispered. "Well done, Ig!"

"Shame they didn't fall asleep any quicker," said Arx, pointing to several jagged holes in the metal around his neck. "Look at these teeth-marks!"

"I'll put the little nuisances safely back in their cave for now." Iggy used his auto-grippers to lift each one and deposit it carefully back inside the hole in the hill.

"Maybe we should go back to the *Sauropod* and ask Admiral Rosso to send a babysitter," said Teggs. "I know the allosaurs are bad, but to take a bunch of little kids in a warship . . ."

"Who cares what YOU think, astro-plop?" A large, fierce grown-up allosaur suddenly jumped into sight at the top of the hill. His brows were blood-red, his teeth were bared and he held a space-rifle in both claws. "We can do whatever we like. *YOU* can't stop us!"

Raising his rifle, he opened fire on the astrosaurs . . .

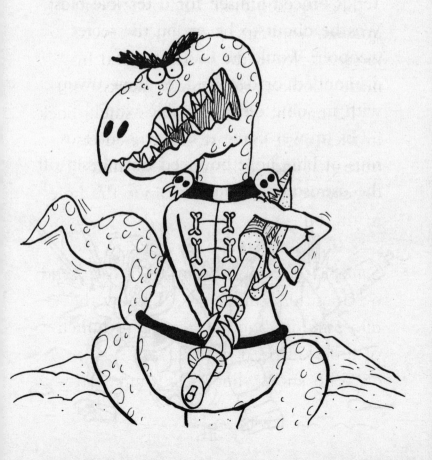

Chapter Four

HIDDEN MENACE

Teggs braced himself for a terrible blast. Was he about to be hit by the secret weapon? Would he find himself dismantled, or dissolved, or done away with in some other horrible way?

His answer came a moment later as rays of blue light bounced harmlessly off the astrosaurs' armour.

"Stun lasers?" Iggy frowned. "Since when do allosaurs use stun lasers?"

"They really must have lost their secret weapons," Arx agreed, shrugging off the attack.

Teggs fired back at the allosaur with his breastplate blasters, but the allosaur had already ducked out of sight.

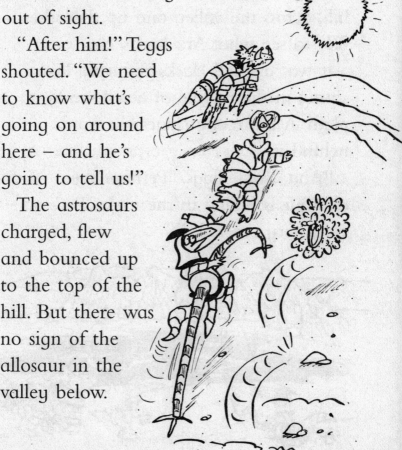

"After him!" Teggs shouted. "We need to know what's going on around here – and he's going to tell us!"

The astrosaurs charged, flew and bounced up to the top of the hill. But there was no sign of the allosaur in the valley below.

Gipsy was puzzled. "Where did it go?"

Arx pointed ahead of them. "I'll take a look from that higher hill. We'll have a better view from there." He zoomed off like a silver missile and landed on the hilltop. Then he quickly signalled to the others. "Quick, over here!"

Teggs, Iggy and Gipsy ran down the hill, across the valley and up the other side to see what Arx had seen.

It was a small, dark, glittering lake, sitting in the middle of a red sandy plain. A big rocky ridge rose up behind it.

"Aha," said Teggs. "Perhaps the allosaur is hiding in the rocks. Let's go – very, very carefully."

The astrosaurs advanced on the
lake in their
mega-tough
armour.
STOMP.
BOMP.
CLOMP.
BOING!
Then
suddenly, the
lake began to
shake. The water
bubbled and foamed.
And with a crash
and splash of
glittering green
liquid – not to
mention a
fearsome,
booming roar –
a gigantic
creature burst
into sight!

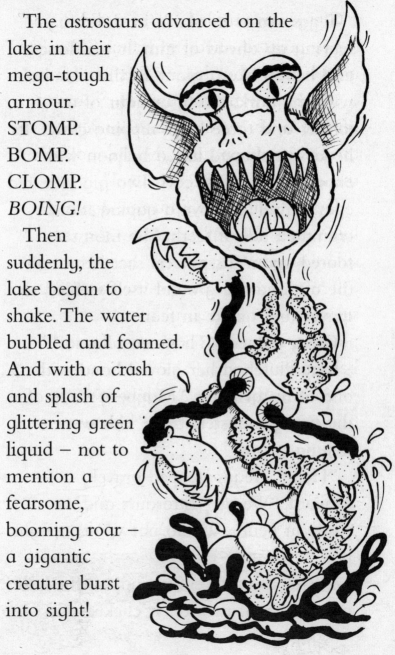

41

Teggs stared in alarm at the thing rearing up ahead of him. It was long and bendy like a giant earthworm, but with the dark, crusty armour of a lobster and three huge nipping claws. Its head was shaped like a balloon with enormous bat-like ears. Two gigantic red eyes swivelled above a gaping mouth crammed full of teeth. The monster roared again. Its pincers sliced through the air, and the ground itself seemed to quiver and quake in fear.

Gipsy gulped. "That's no allosaur!"

Iggy clutched her gloved hand with one of his grippers. "Maybe it's one of the funny monsters those kids were talking about?"

"Hello!" Teggs stepped bravely forward. "We are astrosaurs and we come in peace. We do not want to fight you . . ."

But as the stegosaurus approached, the monster went mental! It clicked and

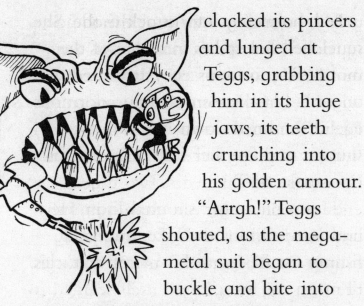

clacked its pincers and lunged at Teggs, grabbing him in its huge jaws, its teeth crunching into his golden armour. "Arrgh!" Teggs shouted, as the mega-metal suit began to buckle and bite into his hide. He fired his tail cannon, but the laser blast bounced off the monster's head without a scratch.

"Don't worry, Captain!" Arx's jet-boots launched him into the air. "I'll pull you free." He grabbed hold of Teggs's tail and tugged like crazy. But the monster clobbered him with a powerful pincer. The triceratops was smashed down into the water with a colossal splash, and vanished from sight.

"Leave my friends alone!" Gipsy

yelled, bouncing into attack mode. She squelched her spikes into one of the monster's enormous eyes. It roared with anger – but then an equally enormous eyelid slammed down like a heavy shutter, trapping her tail. "Oh, no - now I'm stuck too!"

"Hang on, guys," shouted Iggy. He had jumped into the lake, frantically fishing for Arx with his metal tentacles. "I'm on my way."

"So am I!" Arx cried, zipping back out of the water. "Sorry it took me a while to surface – my foot jets fizzled out and I had to restart them."

"Quickly, Arx," Teggs gasped, wriggling with all his strength as the monster's teeth crushed down on his armour even harder. "Never mind me, save Gipsy!"

Arx fired his electro-blasters at the weird monster's eyelid. Thick skin quivered as the current ran through it, then the eyelid flicked open – releasing Gipsy who splashed into the water and bounced straight out again. Iggy caught her in midair with his grippers – until they suddenly melted away to nothing and, with a cry of surprise, Gipsy fell back into the water. "Huh?" Iggy stared in confusion as his armour started to fall apart – forming piles of bits and pieces on the shore. Gipsy quickly swam to the side to join him, unable to believe

her eyes. "It . . . it's just like the robo-rexes and the allosaur spaceship!"

Arx was too busy trying to save his captain to pay attention to Iggy. He crawled into the monster's mouth next to Teggs and strained against its jaws, trying to push them back open . . . until suddenly, his silver armour shimmered and vanished! One moment it was there, the next a heap of metal plates, springs and circuits were falling from his body in a high-tech avalanche, revealing the startled, soaking wet triceratops inside.

Struggling for breath, still trapped in the

monster's jaws, Teggs stared at Arx in alarm. "Your armour has fallen to pieces too!"

But then the monster flicked its head. Teggs was held fast by its terrible teeth, but Arx was not. The triceratops fell out of the giant mouth, falling to the shore below with a heavy thump.

"Arx, Captain!" Gipsy shouted as she and Iggy ran round the lake towards them. "We're coming . . ."

But Teggs could hardly hear her. His in-built snack dispenser burst, filling his helmet with ferns so he couldn't see. Desperately he tried to chomp them

down, but his tummy was so squished he could hardly swallow. And then he realized that the monster was starting to sink back down into the dangerous waters.

"If I'm not squashed or suffocated, I'll drown or disintegrate instead," said Teggs helplessly. "It really looks as though this is the end!"

Chapter Five

THE TIME TERROR

Teggs gasped as the monster's jagged teeth finally tore through his armour, clamping down with crushing force . . .

And as they did so, they must have caused a short circuit in the mega-metal suit's power supply – because a massive surge of energy erupted from the armour! The monster's tongue began to smoke and its teeth turned black. Crackles of power poured through its pincers. Its two red eyes opened and shut as the monster spat Teggs out with incredible force. He went flying through the air like an old tin can and smashed into a sand dune. Then the singed and smoking monster toppled into the water with a thunderous crash, sank beneath the surface and did not re-emerge.

Teggs took off his battered helmet and breathed a sigh of relief to see his three friends running over to join him.

Arx arrived first. "Are you OK, Captain?"

"I feel like an ammonite that's been chewed by a shark," Teggs admitted. "But I'll be all right. How about you?"

"Absolutely fine," Arx declared. "In fact, I'm feeling brilliant."

Gipsy and Iggy came up behind him. "We couldn't keep up with you," Gipsy began. But suddenly her spiky combat armour just dribbled away, making dark, sticky purple puddles on the ground around her. "Oh, no!" she cried in horror. "My lovely spiky armour!"

"It's gone," breathed Arx. "Just like mine and Iggy's. But how?"

Teggs looked at the lake. "The three of you went in the water – but I didn't. And I'm the only one who's still got his armour."

Gipsy shook sludge from her arm and frowned. "You think that the water had something to do with it?"

"It sounds crazy," Teggs agreed. "But just before those test robots disintegrated, I saw someone lean out of the allosaur ship with a bucket . . ."

"I hope it isn't the water," said Iggy slowly. "When Gipsy and I took a dip, our armour kept us perfectly dry. But poor Arx has holes in his suit, so the water will have got inside . . ."

"Nothing wrong with me," Arx insisted, and Teggs had to agree he looked very well indeed. "I feel great, even if my armour's fallen to bits!"

"It's fallen to brand-spanking-*new* bits," said Iggy, holding up a fallen screw and a circuit board. "Just like the allosaur ship."

"I do love a mystery!" said Arx cheerfully, rolling up his wet sleeves. "Let's put all the different bits and pieces together and . . ." He trailed off, staring at his wrist. "That's funny. Where's my scar gone?"

Iggy frowned. "Eh?"

"When we had that run-in with the Star Pirates a year or so back, I was cut by a cutlass in the big fight at the end." He peered at the skin closely. "I've had a scar ever since. Or at least, I *did* have . . ."

"Until you went in that water," said Teggs, studying his friend's arm. "What does it mean?"

Arx gasped, his eyes grew wide, and he sat down with a big thump. Gipsy tried to help him up but he shied away.

"No! Don't touch me!"

Gipsy looked puzzled. "But, I thought you felt fine?"

"I do. In fact I feel years younger," Arx murmured. "And though it sounds unbelievable . . . I think I actually *am*." He shook his big frilly head. "I've got a theory that's completely crackers – but it's the only one that fits."

Teggs saw fear in Arx's eyes. "Let's hear it, old friend."

"*Not* so old, Captain. That's the whole point!" Arx sighed. "I believe that the water in that lake – and the water

thrown over our robots by the allosaur ship – has a very special power. The power to twist time backwards over anything it touches!"

"What?" Iggy spluttered. "But that's impossible."

"Unbelievably unlikely, perhaps," said Arx, still eyeing the place on his wrist where his scar used to be. "But not impossible."

"It's so barmy it actually makes sense," Teggs realized. "The robo-rexes were brand-new creations, so it only took a few splashes of time-water to reverse their history . . ."

"Back to the moment they began as a pile of parts and raw materials," said Gipsy, awestruck.

"And it's the same story with those spaceship parts," Iggy realized. "Just like robots, all spaceships start off as circuits and switches and bits of metal and plastic."

"And what about those allosaur babies?" said Teggs.

"I reckon it wasn't just the ship that was splashed by the time-water," said Arx gravely. "It was the crew too. They've got younger and younger until they've turned into infants."

"Oh, Arx!" A tear welled up in Gipsy's eye. "How long before that happens to you?"

"I don't know." Arx shrugged. "Perhaps it depends on how much water soaks into your body."

Iggy gave a little smile. "You still sound like the same clever old you."

"My body's only lost a few years so far," Arx reminded him. "I'm afraid that the younger my brain becomes, the less

I'll know." He forced a hopeful grin. "Still, I'm older than you three. Perhaps the effect will wear off before I start having to wear nappies!"

"Speaking of things that stink," said Iggy, "what about that big allosaur with the stun laser who ran away? How come *he* wasn't affected?"

"Easy!" came a deep growl from just behind them. "Because he's miles cleverer than any of you!"

Teggs and his friends whirled round to find that very same allosaur on top of the hill behind them, brandishing a space rifle. "I'm Vice-Marshal Frentos,

and these are my troops." A dozen more
of the fierce green carnivores appeared
behind him, armed with death-lasers!
"You have performed most pleasingly,
astrosaurs. Now that you've dealt with
the Guardian of the Time-Water, we
can help ourselves to as much as we
like!" He skipped for joy. "The allosaur
armies shall soon possess bucket-loads of
the greatest weapon in the universe —
and we owe it all to you!"

Chapter Six

ALLOSAUR ATTACK!

Teggs glared at Frentos and his troops,
sniggering away at the top of the hill.
"What are you on about?"

"Let me explain," growled Frentos.
"Only then will you realize what a fool
you have been – and how clever I am.
Because if there's one thing I love in
life, it's a good gloat." He rubbed his
claws together. "A

lovely, lovely
gloat. A gloat
of glory! A
goat? Bah!
But a *gloat* –
hooray!"

"I think we get the idea!" Teggs snapped. "Now, what did you mean, 'Guardian of the Time-Water'? Are you saying that the monster in that lake stops anyone from stealing the stuff?"

Frentos nodded. "It seems unaffected by the time-water. And it squashes anyone who comes too close. Or rather it did, until you defeated it."

"But what good is that water to you?" asked Arx. "Anything that touches it will be twisted back through time."

"We have discovered one substance that is *not* affected," Frentos revealed. "Mega-metal. Its atoms are so old and solid that even time-water can't change them."

My armour's made of mega-metal, Teggs remembered. *If only I had fallen in the time-water and not Arx.*

"Oh. Hang on," said Frentos. "Sorry to interrupt the gloating, but I just need to bark some orders in a loud and unpleasant fashion. Won't be a jiff." He turned to his troops. "Right, you revolting lot! Drop your guns and get busy with the buckets! That water's not going to collect itself. MOVE IT!"

Cringing, the carnivore troops yanked pails from out of their backpacks, rushed down to the lake's glittering edge, and started scooping up the time-water.

"Lucky we allosaurs store our special spaceship fuel in mega-metal buckets, eh?" Frentos sneered. "They make the perfect pails for time-water!"

"But I don't understand," said Gipsy. "We found the baby allosaurs in the remains of your spaceship. How come you and your troops didn't get wet and turn young?"

"Simple – that wasn't *MY* spaceship." Frentos grinned, showing his terrible teeth. "This is such a good part of space for testing top-secret inventions, isn't it? Far from anywhere, quiet and deserted . . ." He sniggered. "We allosaurs have been testing brand-new spaceships that can turn *invisible*." He pulled out a remote and pressed a button – and Teggs gasped as an allosaur ship swam into sight in the next valley, towering over the hill. Scorch marks from the dung torpedoes marked its sides.

Iggy slapped a claw to his forehead. "No wonder we couldn't spot their ship from the shuttle. They'd turned invisible."

"And that's how Frentos seemed to vanish when we chased after him," Gipsy realized. "He ran inside his see-through spaceship, while we ran straight into the Guardian."

Teggs glared at the allosaur. "How did you find out about the time-water in the first place?"

"By total accident," Frentos admitted. "We were testing *two* invisible spaceships here a few days ago to see if they could be seen in super-bright sunlight. Our second ship landed too close to the lake . . ."

Iggy raised an eyebrow. "And the Guardian attacked, right?"

"Yes," Frentos agreed. "The crew were splashed as they escaped and so was their ship. No sooner had they taken off than the ship fell apart – and the crew began to get younger . . ."

"How terrible," said Gipsy sadly.

"Terrible?" Frentos spluttered. "It was brilliant! I knew straight away that I, Vice-Marshal Frentos, had chanced upon the most incredible weapon in the universe!"

"But to get it, you had to beat the Guardian," Teggs realized. "And since you and your troops weren't tough enough, you got us to do it for you."

"When we scanned the area and found you foolish astrosaurs were close by, we couldn't believe our luck!" Frentos smirked.

"I made the time-twisted crew wring out their wet clothes into a mega-metal bucket so I had just enough time-water to get your attention."

Iggy nodded gravely. "You trashed our robots to make us come after you. Since they were brand-new, they vanished in a flash."

"And now you've so kindly dealt with the Guardian, the time-water's all ours!" Frentos threw back his brutish head and laughed. "Think what I can do with it! Some good-sized squirts could unravel a fleet of spaceships . . . A cupful in a planet's water supply could turn the entire population into helpless babes, allowing us to invade without firing a single shot . . ."

"Thinking of it is all you'll do, ugly-nose!" said Arx hotly. "'Cos we're going to stop you. Right, Captain?"

Teggs turned to him, and got a shock. Already, Arx had grown much younger. He looked smaller, darker green and had shorter horns.

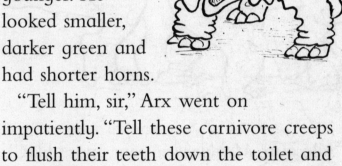

"Tell him, sir," Arx went on impatiently. "Tell these carnivore creeps to flush their teeth down the toilet and push off!"

"Oh, dear." Gipsy's head-crest was turning the bluest Teggs had ever seen it. "Captain, Arx is turning into a hot-headed teenager!"

"You think you're so tough." Arx marched up to Vice-Marshal Frentos.

"Allosaur? *Marshmallow*-saur, more like!"

Frentos gave a angry roar. "No one speaks to me like that when I'm gloating and lives." He pulled his death-laser from his belt holster and pointed it at Arx. "You won't have to worry about growing any younger, triceratops. It is time you died *NOW!*"

Chapter Seven

CAVE OF DANGER

"It's time you shut up, you mean," cried Arx – and butted Frentos in the stomach! The allosaur leader doubled over and dropped the gun. Then Arx swatted him with his tail and shoved him over backwards. "Take that, burger-breath!"

"Good work, Arx," Teggs cried.

But the other allosaur troops were already setting down their heavy buckets and grabbing for their guns. Teggs checked his leg-lasers – one was chewed and bent but there was just a little energy left in the other. He fired at the nearest buckets, knocking them over and sending time-water pouring everywhere.

The allosaur troops jumped about like street-dancers in a panic, desperate not to get their feet wet. A few more laser-blasts and the allosaurs were running for cover over the hill.

Arx blew a raspberry at them. "And don't come back!"

"I'm afraid they will,' said Teggs. "And we've got no way to call the *Sauropod* to get reinforcements."

"We'd better head for the shuttle," said Iggy.

"And ask Admiral Rosso to send a space doctor for poor Arx," Gipsy added.

"You'll ALL need a doctor by the time I'm through with you," Frentos roared. He picked up his death-laser and started firing wildly.

"Look out!" Teggs jumped in front of his friends as searing death rays started zinging about. His damaged armour took the brunt of the gunfire until he cocked his leg and opened fire again, driving the angry allosaur back into cover.

"This leg-laser's almost had it," Teggs muttered, noting the smoking nozzle.

"Get ready to run, guys. I'll shield you all as best I can."

"If I shrink much smaller," moaned Arx, "you'll be able to carry me in your helmet!"

"Don't worry, Arx," said Teggs. "Somehow we'll get you back to normal again." He let loose one last laser bolt — but it barely sizzled. "OK, it's time to go. Everybody — RUN!"

The astrosaurs raced up the hillside towards Frentos and his men. "Shoot them down," the carnivore yelled. Soon, a barrage of beams from the allosaur troops started zinging all around them. Teggs gasped as his ragged armour shook and rattled, but didn't slow down. He barged Frentos aside with a resounding CLANG! Then he and his friends were over the hilltop and racing back towards the shuttle in the blazing heat.

But the allosaur army were soon on their tails.

"I'll give them a *real* target," Arx volunteered. "Look at me go — *wheeeeeeeee!*" Before anyone could argue, he galloped away like a prehistoric pony, zigzagging wildly across the plain as explosions went off all around him. But then more allosaurs  swarmed out of their spaceship, and as the gunfire grew greater, Arx was forced back to join the others.

"We'll never make it to the shuttle at this rate," Iggy panted.

"Perhaps we can hide in the baby raptors' cave and give Frentos the slip?" Gipsy suggested.

"It's worth a try," Teggs said.

"Caves! Brilliant!" Young Arx beamed, hardly out of breath. "I love caves, Captain. Let's explore now! Can we?" Then he frowned. "Er . . . what were we looking for again?"

Teggs looked helplessly at Gipsy and Iggy. "Arx was right – as his body grows younger, his mind gets younger too. He's not thinking like an astrosaur any more. He's more like a keen little kid!"

The astrosaurs climbed the second hill and tumbled down the other side. The scraps of the first carnivore craft lay scattered all around – and there was the hole in the hillside.

"It's too small for us to get through," Gipsy wailed.

"But not for me," said Arx. He dashed inside and started bashing away at bits of the entrance with his horns, making it

wider and wider until Teggs, Gipsy and
Iggy were able to squeeze through into
the gloomy cave.

"Try not to wake the allo-tykes,"
Teggs whispered.

But then Iggy gasped. "There's . . .
there's no one to wake."

As Teggs's eyes grew accustomed to
the darkness, he saw that in some
impossible time-twisting way the baby
carnivores had all turned into eggs!

"The 'growing younger' effect must
speed up as time goes by," said Iggy
grimly.

As he spoke, Gipsy caught sight of movement at the back of the cave. "Hey!" she hissed. "Who's there?"

"Er . . . no one," came the deep, husky reply.

"We mean no harm," warbled a female voice, croaky with age. "We have given food and water to the little toothy ones, since their Vice-Marshal abandoned them."

"Aha," said Gipsy nervously. "So *you're* the 'monsters' the little beasts mentioned before."

"Yes." The female sighed. "But now, I'm afraid, they need us no longer."

"Captain, can you put the lights on?" Arx's voice was high and shrill like a child's. "I'm scared of the dark!"

"Very well," said the first voice. "One moment . . ."

A green lantern switched on, lighting the cave with a queasy glow. The astrosaurs gaped in amazement at the two alien creatures before them. Young Arx leaped into Gipsy's arms, stammering and sucking his thumb. "W-w-what are *they*?"

The creatures were greyish-blue, with small, shrunken bodies and big, domed heads. Their skinny arms ended in strange shovel-like hands. One had an enormous white beard that almost covered his three spindly legs. The other had long white hair that hung down all the way to her extraordinarily long toenails.

"We are astrosaurs," said Teggs calmly. "Who are you?"

"I am Humm," said the bearded stranger. "This is Jingal. We are part of a planet-survey team from the next galaxy. I am a scientist . . ."

"And I am an explorer," Jingal added. "Our scanners detected an ultra-rare substance here, so we decided to investigate . . ."

Teggs nodded. "Let me guess – you wandered too near the lake and a big monster came out?"

"Almost," said Humm. "While burying our spaceship beneath the planet's surface as usual – we don't like to draw attention to ourselves – the vibrations woke the monster. He wormed his way down here and attacked us."

"And as he did so, time-water leaked out from the bottom of the lake," Jingal explained. "We managed to escape the Guardian, but the water splashed all over us."

"Very chilly it was too." Humm shivered. "You feel the cold at our age."

Iggy seemed puzzled. "I don't want to be rude, but surely YOU can't be getting any younger? You look so old."

"Cheek," Jingal huffed.

"The time-water has affected us differently," Humm explained. "It has twisted our timelines to make us terribly old – thousands of years older than we were!"

"Wow!" Teggs boggled. "You live for ages."

"But we can't last much longer," sighed Jingal. "We have been working on a cure for the time-twisting in our underground spaceship. But it is not easy. The water destroys our equipment."

Humm nodded sadly. "So we potter about and wait for our end . . ."

"You mustn't give up!" Gipsy urged them. "The time-water has turned you two older but it's made poor Arx turn younger. If we knew why, perhaps we could get all of you back to normal?"

"Yes, my armour is made from mega-metal," Teggs told them. "You can use the helmet as a bucket – it should contain the time-water for as many tests as you need."

Humm chewed on the end of his beard. "Well . . . I suppose we could try again."

But just then, there was a scraping noise outside the cave mouth. "All right, astro-scum!" Frentos's vile voice echoed around the cave. "We know you're in there – your tracks lead inside."

"Oh, no!" Gipsy whispered. "Now what do we do?"

"I will give you to the count of five to come out and let me finish gloating over you," Frentos went on. "Otherwise, we shall fire our weapons into this cave and destroy you all." He cleared his throat. "One . . . two . . ."

Young Arx buried his head in Gipsy's shoulder, while the other astrosaurs swapped hopeless looks. "He's got us trapped," said Teggs. "And we can't risk Humm and Jingal getting hurt. I hate to say it, but we'll just have to surrender."

Iggy nodded bitterly. "Surrender — or die!"

Chapter Eight

TIME RUNNING OUT

Outside the cave, Frentos was still counting. "Three!" he growled. "Um . . . what comes after three again?"

"Astrosaurs," whispered Humm. "There is another way out of this cave. We built a tunnel here from our spaceship so the monster couldn't see us come and go."

Teggs grinned. "Perfect!"

"Four," called Frentos. "Yes, that comes after three. And after four . . ."

"Quickly!" Waving her spade-like hands, Jingal ushered them towards a large crack in the rear of the cave. "This is the way."

"But Frentos and his allosaur troops will come straight after us," Iggy realized as he squeezed through the gap. "It won't take them long to work out where we've gone."

"If only we could hold them off somehow . . ." said Gipsy.

"Arx go plop-plop!" came a squeaky voice.

"He's turned younger still," Teggs groaned. "Now he's just a baby."

"Plop-plop," baby Arx insisted. Gipsy quickly held him away from her as his little green bum got busy, producing quite a pile of dung.

"Ugh!" Iggy choked. "I'd forgotten how toxic baby dino-dung can be."

Another dozen dollops flopped out, and Teggs's eyes started streaming. "His bottom's unstoppable!"

Baby Arx giggled naughtily.

"FIVE!" roared Frentos, as his forces marched right up to the cave mouth. Teggs bundled the others towards Humm and Jingal's exit, but knew they could never get away in time. "Stand by to fire, lads . . . URGH! What is that whiff? Ooof, my nose . . ."

The sound of carnivores coughing and spluttering and dropping their guns carried from outside as the disgusting dung-pong blew from the cave.

"Get going," Teggs told Gipsy.

She patted Arx on the head as she went. "Even as a baby, he's still getting us out of trouble."

Baby Arx grinned up at Teggs. "Mama?"

Teggs frowned. "It's definitely time to leave!"

The astrosaurs followed the aliens through a rough tunnel lit by luminous mushrooms. Teggs shivered – it was freezing cold down here, away from the fierce sunlight. In the distance he could hear groans and wheezes as Frentos forced his soldiers into the cave. Quickly, Teggs struggled out of his broken armour and used everything but the helmet to build a barricade, blocking the tunnel to slow down the allosaurs. Then he caught up with the others beside a pair of

large white doors – the entrance to
Humm and Jingal's
underground spaceship.

"Please excuse
the mess,"
said

Humm,
tottering inside on
his three grey-blue legs.
"We weren't expecting visitors."
Teggs frowned at the state of the
spaceship. From floor to ceiling it was a
jumbled mess of scientific bric-a-brac.
Every available surface was smothered
in tools and gadgets Teggs had never
seen before, together with jars and

beakers almost overflowing with smelly chemical stews.

"It looks like you've been working hard to find a cure," Iggy observed.

"Yes, indeed," Humm agreed. "Although actually, a lot of this mess comes from my experiments to find the perfect warm drink."

Jingal nodded. "At our age you like a nice warm drink."

"Ooh, you do, Jingal, you do," Humm agreed.

Teggs looked anxiously at baby Arx,

who was staring about with interest. How long did they have before he became an egg? "Er, do you have any samples of the time-water?"

"There's a drip coming through the roof over here," said Humm, walking stiffly over to another door. He opened it to reveal a short passage, where the water was trickling down from the ceiling to the sandy ground. "We're under the lake, of course. The leak started soon after we started digging, so we switched to the other tunnel instead."

Teggs passed Humm his crumpled helmet. "Where do you think the time-water and its Guardian came from?"

"Who knows?" said the shrivelled-up alien, carefully collecting the mysterious liquid in the helmet.

"Perhaps a mighty space pirate hid the time-water here and left a savage pet to guard it," Jingal suggested.

Humm nodded. "Or, perhaps time-water forms when a pool of rare chemicals cooks in solar radiation for billions of years – and the Guardian grew there over the centuries. On the other hand, maybe the time-water is—"

"Wee-wee," said baby Arx suddenly.

Humm shook his head. "No, I don't think it's wee-wee."

"*Arx* go wee-wee," chirped the little triceratops.

"Oh no!" Iggy groaned.

"Get something to catch it in, quickly!" said Gipsy. The next moment, baby Arx started weeing like a water fountain straight into the air. Iggy grabbed an old bucket and ran around trying to catch the torrent as best he could.

"Don't let that widdle spoil our sample of time-water!" Teggs grabbed the half-full helmet and shielded it with his chest. "We *must* work out the differences between your species and ours, Humm. Maybe then we'll understand why you and Jingal have got older while Arx and the allosaur crew have got younger."

"Well . . . Jingal and I only eat plants," said Humm.

"So do we," Teggs replied. "But the allosaurs eat meat, so it can't be that."

"We have scaly skin, but yours is wrinkly," Iggy suggested, putting down a very full bucket.

Gipsy nodded. "Er . . . we have tails and you don't."

"We can blow bubbles with our

toes," said Jingal.

"There must be hundreds of differences," Teggs groaned. "And no time to find out which one matters." He clonked his makeshift mega-metal cauldron down on the table. "What are we going to do?"

Baby Arx looked over at the despairing stegosaurus. "Mama!" he squeaked. Suddenly, he wriggled out of

Gipsy's grip and jumped toward Teggs – but missed and landed right in the armoured helmet!

"NO!" Teggs yelled as the triceratops made a splash. "That thing's full of time-water!"

Jingal hid her eyes. "If your friend wasn't doomed before, he will be finished now for sure . . ."

Chapter Nine

AGE ALARM

Iggy and Gipsy rushed up beside Teggs, staring down at the helmet in horror. Baby Arx had disappeared. Now, there was only an egg rolling about in the time-water.

"Arx," whispered Gipsy, tears brimming in her eyes. "Oh, poor Arx . . ."

But suddenly, the helmet exploded –
as something large and bright green shot
out from inside! Gipsy yelled, and Teggs
and Iggy jumped back in alarm . . .

To find a familiar, full-size triceratops
standing in front of them!

"What?" Teggs gasped. "Arx, is it
really you? Are you OK?"

"I'm not sure. Everything is so

hazy . . ." Arx blinked, looked around –
and blushed. "Hey, I've got no
clothes on!"

"But apart from that, you're back to

normal!" cried Gipsy. "Fantastic!"

"It sure is," Iggy agreed, clapping him on the back.

But Humm and Jingal were cowering away behind a desk. "Er, I hate to be a spoilsport," said Humm. "But there was quite a lot of time-water in that helmet, remember?"

Gipsy looked down at her damp uniform. "It's splashed all over us!"

Teggs realized his face was soaking wet – and Iggy's top was dripping. "Oh, no!" Iggy groaned.

"I'm so sorry," wailed Arx. "What happened? How did you cure me?"

"It wasn't us," Teggs admitted. "You jumped in the water, turned into an egg

– and suddenly, time twisted you back."

"And now it will turn us into babies too," said Gipsy, her head-crest glowing white with shock. "I feel funny. It must be happening already . . ."

Arx walked up to her and frowned. "I don't think you're getting any younger . . ." He swung round to look at Teggs and Iggy – and jumped in the air in alarm. "In fact, you're getting *older*!"

"*What*?" Teggs looked at his reflection in the back of a metal tray.

It was true – his face was starting to wrinkle. Iggy's brown scales were growing paler. Gipsy was beginning to stoop.

"It's happening to you like it happened to us," Jingal realized, her wrinkled grey-blue face full of sadness. "But why? Your friend and the toothy ones all became younger."

Teggs thought harder than he'd ever thought before. "We were trying to find differences between you and us to explain the time-water working differently," he muttered. "But perhaps we should think about differences in the time-water itself . . ."

Iggy scratched his head, but Gipsy got

what he was driving at. "Arx and the allosaurs were splashed with water from the top of the lake, but Jingal and Humm were splashed with water from the *bottom* of the lake."

Arx nodded slowly. "When I fell in the water it was hot from the sunshine."

"But Humm said the water that splashed him and Jingal was cold," Iggy remembered. "Right, Humm?"

"Freezing," Humm agreed, pointing over to the little trickle of time-water in the tunnel. "That stuff has seeped through old, cold rocks a long way from any sunlight."

"So it's the *temperature* of the water that matters," Teggs breathed. "Maybe that's how the Guardian survives in the lake – it moves between hot and cold time-water to stay the same age!"

Gipsy nodded. "So if we can just get back to the surface and splash ourselves with warm water—"

"We should get back to normal!" Iggy jumped in the air – and pulled a muscle in his hip. "Ow! I was forgetting, I'm not as young as I was."

"So what are we waiting for?" said Gipsy. "Let's go!" She bustled over to the door and threw it open . . .

To reveal Vice-Marshal Frentos in the doorway, his terrifying troops crowding behind him! He roared and lunged for Gipsy, claws bared . . .

Arx sprinted forwards and slammed the door shut with a butt of his horns. "Not today, thank you!"

"Let me in, astro-fools," snarled Frentos.

"So you can gloat at us again?" Teggs jeered through the door. "I don't think so. We really haven't the time."

Frentos growled in warning. "I don't know who's helping you, but I'll scrunch them too unless you surrender straight away."

"Forget it," Humm shouted. "You'll scrunch us anyway, you big toothy bully."

"It was awful of you, leaving those little ones all alone," Jingal added. "You should be ashamed."

"I've had enough of this," said Frentos. "We got past your stinky dung. We knocked down your barricade. Now we'll smash our way in there and make you sorry you were ever hatched. Ready, lads? GET TO IT!"

A loud THUMP shook the sturdy doors.

Teggs turned to Humm and Jingal. "Is there another way out of here?"

Humm shook his head sadly and pointed to the trickle of time-water. "Only into the cave through there."

"Do you have any weapons?" asked Iggy.

"No," said Jingal. "We're explorers, not soldiers."

BANG! The doors almost wobbled off their hinges.

"There must be something we can do!" Gipsy cried. "If you were still an infant, Arx, your dung might distract them again."

Iggy grimaced. "Instead, all we've got is a big bucket full of baby wee."

"Wait," said Teggs, lifting up the brimming bucket. "That might just be enough."

"What?" Gipsy peered at Teggs. "Captain, you haven't lost your marbles already, have you?"

Teggs opened his mouth to reply – but then, with an almighty *WHUMP*, the doors crashed open. Biting and snapping, the slavering allosaur hordes forced their way inside . . .

Chapter Ten

GO JUMP IN THE LAKE!

Frentos glared round at astrosaurs and
aliens alike, roaring and ready to
pounce. But Teggs calmly raised the
bucket and sloshed him with baby Arx's
wee! The other allosaurs stopped rigid
as Teggs splashed all of them as well.

"Bleurgh!" Frentos spat. "What was that?"

Teggs smiled. "Just a bit of time-water, that's all."

"WHAT?" Frentos bellowed with rage and raised his deadly claws. "I shall destroy you for this!"

"You'd better be quick." Teggs ducked the attack and splashed even more wee over him and his troops. "You're getting younger and younger now – and only we can cure you."

"Right," said Gipsy, playing along with her captain's trick. "So you'd better put down your guns and do as we say."

"We need to get back to the lake," Teggs went on. "And quickly."

"The lake?" Frentos was scarlet with rage. "You are lying. There *is* no cure."

"Oh?" Arx strode boldly up to Frentos. "Just look at me!"

"You? But . . . but you were splashed," Frentos stammered. "I saw you getting younger." He grabbed Humm by the throat. "Tell me the truth. How did this triceratops reverse the twist of time?"

Humm pointed to the trickle of time-water dripping down beyond the other door. "If you must know, he took a bath in some of that stuff over there . . ."

"Quick!" Frentos shoved Humm aside and charged towards the cold dripping time-water. His panic-stricken troops crowded in after him, desperate to get wet too.

"I really wouldn't do that if I were you," Teggs warned him. "It will make you old and wrinkly."

"Yeah, right, of course it will," Frentos sneered. "You're trying to trick us. Well, as soon as we've cleaned up here, we're going to get you . . ."

"There's no telling some people," said

Teggs. "Come on, everyone!"

Jingal and Humm led the way, and the astrosaurs followed them as quickly as they could. But for Teggs, Iggy and Gipsy old age was setting in fast. Teggs felt stiff and wobbly all over. Iggy kept bumping into things as his eyesight grew blurred. And Gipsy was panting for breath after only a few moments' running.

Arx gently nudged his friends onwards. They *had* to reach the lake of time-water before it was too late.

"Hey!" came a distant shriek from Frentos. "We really *are* getting wrinkly. Just wait till I get my claws on those astrosaurs . . ."

"Now the allosaurs will chase us all the way back to the lake," Humm realized.

Teggs nodded, rubbing his aching back. "If they calm down we can cure them for real."

"First, we'd better cure ourselves," wheezed Gipsy.

Limping, hobbling, staggering and stumbling, the stricken astrosaurs and their friends finally made it out onto the baking surface of the tiny planet. Teggs and Iggy had grown incredibly wrinkly. Gipsy was starting to look like a stripy green prune. Jingal and Humm leaned on each other as they waddled along.

And all the time, Arx kept them moving.
"Come on, you can make it … It's not
far to the other side of the
valley … Keep up and keep together …
Just one more hillside …"

Finally, hot, bothered and gasping for
breath, Teggs reached the top of the
slope. "I'm over the hill in more ways
than one," he puffed. "But at
least we got here." He gazed
out over the lake, which was
glittering darkly in the glare
of the giant sun.

"Thank space for that," gasped old Iggy, squinting in the sunlight. "What are those little golden things down on the plain?"

"Buckets of time-water," said Granny Gipsy. "The allosaur troops dumped them there before they chased us."

"I'll fetch one," Arx volunteered. He rushed off down the slope, found a full bucket, and brought it back. "There. But you'd better be careful – it was sheer luck that I soaked up enough cold time-water to twist me back to  my normal age – give or take a year or two. So splash on a little at a time – or you could end up *too* young."

"Let me help you, Gipsy." Teggs sloshed his friend with a little of the warm water. Gipsy splashed him back, and each drop made his scaly skin tingle. Then she shook her wet hooves over Iggy.

"I wonder how long it will take?" said Teggs impatiently.

Jingal and Humm had grabbed some more buckets – and were emptying them all over themselves. "Well, after all," said Humm, "we've got two thousand years of twisted time to roll back!"

Suddenly, a laser bolt sizzled past Teggs's head. He turned to find an elderly army of grey, stooped allosaur troops coming closer. Some of them seemed very shrivelled, using their rusty guns as walking sticks. Frentos himself was looking extra-rotten and wrinkled, kicking and shoving his soldiers up the hillside and firing his weapon into the air.

"Uh-oh," said Humm and Jingal in unison.

"Forget the fighting, Frentos," Arx called. "A quick dip in some warm time-water is the only cure for that cold shower you took."

"Pah! You must think I'm stupid." Frentos let rip with his death-laser and his troops did the same. "You'll pay for ruining my plans!"

A blistering barrage of laser bolts filled the air around the astrosaurs. They dragged Humm and Jingal out of range

over the crest of the hill, and then started to run down towards the time-water.

"The only cover is those rocks on the far side of the lake," Teggs realized. "We must try to reach them." But the time-water was making him feel dizzy. He saw Jingal and Humm run onward, taking the lead — but couldn't keep up. Iggy and Gipsy were finding it hard to run too. They stumbled to the ground — which started to shake.

"Not again," groaned Arx. "The Guardian of the Lake — it's waking up!"

Sure enough, the hideous head of the giant wormy monster was starting to push through the dark surface of the weird waters.

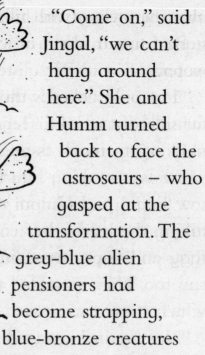

"Come on," said Jingal, "we can't hang around here." She and Humm turned back to face the astrosaurs – who gasped at the transformation. The grey-blue alien pensioners had become strapping, blue-bronze creatures with smooth, handsome faces. "Here – let us give you a lift."

To Teggs's amazement, Jingal lifted him up into the air with her large, flat hands and hefted him away. Humm did the same for Iggy, while Arx placed Gipsy on his back and galloped away after the two aliens. Beside them, the Guardian writhed and wriggled as it reared out of the time-water and turned towards them, growling with menace . . .

But then a storm of laser beams peppered its tough, glistening skin. The Guardian shrieked with anger and whirled round to face Frentos and his doddering troops as they stormed over the hill.

Clinging onto Jingal as she reached the shelter of the rocks, Teggs saw Frentos fire at the monster again and again. "Who needs armoured astrosaurs?" the vice-marshal screeched. "Who needs to be young and fit? We can beat this monster all by ourselves – right, lads?"

But his troops' only reply was a wail of despair as the monster swooped down towards them. With a swipe of its pincers, it knocked the whole lot of them into the lake. The cruel carnivores struggled and splashed in the churning black waters, slowly slipping under, vanishing from sight . . .

"Hey, I think the warm time-water's working," Iggy said excitedly. "I can see properly again!"

"My face is getting smoother," Gipsy said excitedly.

"My aches and pains are fading." Teggs grinned. "I'm starting to feel young again!"

Arx smiled. "I wonder how young Frentos and his troops will soon be feeling?"

 Several long minutes bubbled by as the astrosaurs watched and waited. At last, thirty or so large speckled eggs

popped up to the surface of the lake. With a dismissive sweep of its tail, the monster knocked the eggs out of the water and onto the shore. Then, with a purr of satisfaction, it plunged back beneath the waters and was lost from sight.

Teggs blinked. "It's gone."

Gipsy nodded. "And those evil allosaurs have been well taken care of."

"While we are finally back to our normal, dashing young selves," said Iggy with a grin.

"So are we!" said Humm, grabbing Jingal in a massive hug.

"Now we

can fix up our spaceship and travel back to our own galaxy." Jingal beamed. "And it's all thanks to you four."

Teggs saluted them both. "We could never have won through without your help."

"Very true," Arx agreed. "But, Captain, I do have two small questions. First – what are we going to do with all the allosaur eggs?"

"Send them back to Allosauria for hatching," Teggs decided. "Let Frentos and his troops grow up all over again. Perhaps this time they might turn out a little nicer."

"What's your second question, Arx?" Gipsy wondered.

"How much time-water do you think we should take back to Admiral Rosso?" The triceratops grinned. "It's the scientific discovery of a lifetime! Just think – with a few warm drops you

122

could recycle just about anything. Or with a few cold drops you could turn seeds into trees in two seconds flat and feed millions . . ."

But Teggs was shaking his head. "Sorry, Arx. I think we should leave the time-water right where it is, and never breathe a word about it to anyone."

"It is simply too dangerous for any race to possess," Humm agreed.

"Oh." Arx sighed. "I suppose you're right. But what if someone else comes here?"

"I know! The allosaur ship!" cried Iggy. "It can turn itself invisible thanks to some gadget on board, right? Well, with a bit of fiddling, I bet I can boost its power. We can turn this whole *planet* invisible!"

"So the Guardian can live in peace, out of sight, with no more unwelcome visitors." Gipsy nodded happily. "That's a brilliant idea!"

"And I've had a brilliant idea too," said Teggs. "As soon as Iggy's done that, let's get back to the *Sauropod* for another adventure." He grinned. "Because, give or take the odd twist of time, you're only young once — so let's not waste a single madcap, marvellous moment!"

THE END
The Astrosaurs will return in
THE SABRE-TOOTH SECRET

ASTRO PUZZLE TIME

THE TWIST OF TIME
QUIZ Questions

1. What is Teggs's new super-swish space armour made from?

2. What's the one thing in life that Vice-Marshal Frentos really, really loves?

3. What's so special about the Allosaurs' spaceship?

4. Who did the astrosaurs meet when they hid inside the cave?

5. Teggs pretended to soak the allosaurs with time-water – but what was really in the bucket?

Answers:

1. Maxi-strength mega-metal
2. Gloating over his captured enemies!
3. It can turn invisible
4. Humm and Jingal, two alien beings
5. Baby Arx's wee!

ASTRO PUZZLE TIME

TIME-TWISTER

A few drops of time-water must have splashed over this book – the timeline of the story below has been muddled up! Sort through the nine events and put them in the right order.

1. Arx was turned back to normal by cold time-water – but accidentally splashed Teggs, Gipsy and Iggy, who began to grow older.

2. An allosaur ship attacked them and led them to a strange planet.

4. While fighting the monster, Arx was splashed by the time-water and started turning younger.

7. The astrosaurs found a massive monster in a weird lake and had to fight it.

9.Teggs, Iggy, Gipsy and the aliens escaped to the lake and used warm time-water to make themselves young again.

6.Finally, the Guardian got rid of the evil allosaurs by turning them into eggs.

3.The allosaurs revealed they had tricked Teggs and his crew into defeating the monster so they could steal its time-water to use as a weapon.

8.Escaping the allosaurs, Teggs, Gipsy, Iggy and baby Arx met two old aliens in a cave.

5.In the beginning, the astrosaurs were testing out some top-secret super-armour.

☐ ☐ ☐ ☐ ☐ ☐ ☐ ☐ ☐ ☐

Answer:

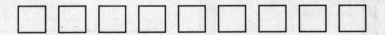
5-2-7-4-3-8-1-9-6

Visit www.**stevecolebooks**.co.uk for fun, games, jokes, to meet the characters and much, much more!

Welcome to a world where dinosaurs fly spaceships and cows use a time-machine . . .

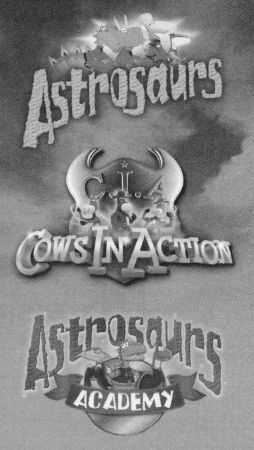

Sign up for the Steve Cole monthly newsletter to find out what your favourite author is up to!